Our Teacher Is A Fish!

Always reach for your dreams!
Jo Ann Fisher

JoAnn Fischer

Inspired by my two granddaughters,
Kaylee Ruth and Sophia Rachael,
and all my future grandchildren

It was a beautiful spring morning. Mrs. Fisher was now an old woman looking out of her large kitchen window gazing upon the beautiful flowers blossoming, trees blooming and birds singing. It made her feel happy and that made her think back to the time when she was a young woman and how life had taken her on many exciting adventures.

It all began with her husband Mr. Fisher who was a teacher at an elementary school in the town Mrs. Fisher lived in. But the big surprise that I must tell you is that Mrs. Fisher was a FISH! That is right. Mrs. Fisher was a fish that lived in a fish tank in a pet store in town. Mr. Fisher would visit the fish store every day and began to love the beauty of one of the fishes in the fish tank. It was a fish of many colors-orange, pink, green, blue, and yellow.

He bought the beautiful fish and brought it to his classroom for his fish tank. The children loved the fish. They would feed it everyday and sometimes clean out the tank. They were very careful with the fish that lived inside of it.

One day early in the morning, Mr. Fisher came into the classroom before the students arrived. He saw this beautiful lady with a dress of many colors sitting in a puddle of water in his classroom. He was startled! "Who are you?" he asked. She replied, "I am the colorful fish from your fish tank. I was given love by all of you, and I wanted to hug you all very much. I kept wishing and wishing, so last night I jumped out of the fish tank and fell on the floor and became a woman!" Mr. Fisher was so happy.

When the children came in that morning and heard the news they were delighted and gave their new friend a big hug. Mr. Fisher loved her very much. In fact, he loved her so much he married her, and they were very happy together.

Mrs. Fisher became a Kindergarten teacher. Her students loved her class because outside the classroom door she had a sign that read, "Fish Stories Told Here". She told her students many exciting fish adventures. They did not know that she was the fish in the exciting stories she told.

The children were inspired by Mrs. Fisher's stories. They would draw the most beautiful pictures of fish and adventures in the sea.

One day Mrs. Fisher told the children in her class something very special that she didn't tell everyone. She became a fish in the summertime! They were amazed.

The school year was coming to an end. When Mrs. Fisher wasn't teaching in the summer, she went to visit her family in the sea. Mr. Fisher would take her to the bay by the ocean where she was born and tell her that he loved her and would miss her. She then would start swimming in the bay, and as she entered the ocean, she turned into a fish once more. She was so happy to see her fish family. She loved them very much.

One day a little boy named Jonas was fishing on a boat in the ocean with his dad. He wanted to catch a fish and bring it home so his mom and sisters would be proud of him. All of a sudden he was holding on tight to his fishing pole. It was tugging and jerking and almost pulled him into the sea. He finally pulled really hard and was able to get the fish into the boat.

The fish was so beautiful and full of many different colors. Jonas was so excited. He couldn't wait to bring it home. As he tried to get the fish off the hook something came over him. He sensed compassion and love for the fish. He realized he didn't want the fish to die. Jonas looked at the fish and wondered if the fish he caught was Mrs. Fisher.

You see Jonas had been in Mrs. Fisher's kindergarten class, and he remembered the story she had told to the class. It was hard for Jonas to throw the fish back into the ocean, because he wanted his mom and sisters to be proud of him. But the love and respect he had for his teacher was greater than the joy of bringing a fish home that day. So Jonas decided to gently throw the colorful fish back into the ocean.

September came and school was soon to begin. Mr. Fisher returned to the bay hoping that Mrs. Fisher would come home to him safe. As Mrs. Fisher swam from the ocean as a fish into the bay, she changed into a woman once more. Mr. Fisher saw her and was so happy. They missed each other very much.

When they returned to teach their classes, Mrs. Fisher saw Jonas in the hallway at school. She stopped and thanked Jonas and told him that she was the fish that he had caught and then let go. Jonas was amazed. He was happy to see that Mrs. Fisher returned back to school safe from the danger of the sea.

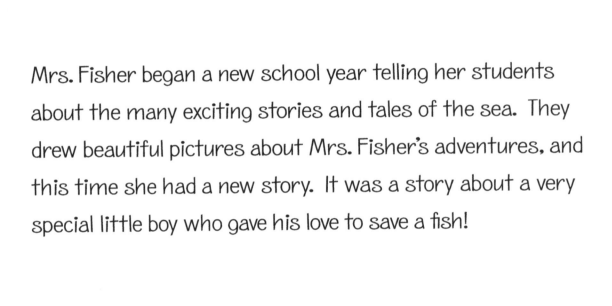

Mrs. Fisher began a new school year telling her students about the many exciting stories and tales of the sea. They drew beautiful pictures about Mrs. Fisher's adventures, and this time she had a new story. It was a story about a very special little boy who gave his love to save a fish!